Mr Wolf and Enormous Turnip

Jan Fearnley

DEAN

First published in Great Britain 2004 by Egmont UK Limited
This edition published 2019 by Dean,
an imprint of Egmont UK Limited,
The Yellow Building, 1 Nicholas Road, London W11 4AN

www.egmont.co.uk

Text and illustrations copyright © 2004 Jan Fearnley

Jan Fearnley has asserted her moral rights

ISBN 978 0 6035 7758 1
70741/001
Printed in Malaysia

A CIP catalogue record for this title is available from the British Library.

One day, Mr Wolf found a most
peculiar thing in his garden.
It was a great big enormous turnip.

"Yum, yum!" he said,
licking his lips at the thought
of spicy turnip stew for supper.

He rubbed his paws together and set about picking the turnip.

But even though he *pulled* and *tugged,*
the turnip would not move.
Suddenly, a croaky little voice called out from
behind the bushes.
"Won't somebody help me, please?"

It was a little frog.
And he had a very sad tale to tell.

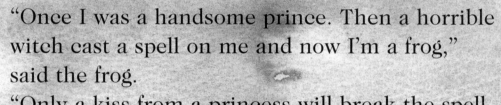

"Once I was a handsome prince. Then a horrible witch cast a spell on me and now I'm a frog," said the frog.
"Only a kiss from a princess will break the spell. Please help."

Mr Wolf's tummy rumbled long and loud.
He looked at the turnip.

"If you help me," said the frog, noticing Mr Wolf's hesitation, "I'll command my servants to pull up your turnip."

"What a nice little frog," thought Mr Wolf. "I'll do what I can."

Mr Wolf took the frog to the royal palace where the beautiful princesses lived.

"I'm sure we can persuade a princess to kiss you better," he said.

They found the first princess in a royal chamber.
Minstrels serenaded her with sweet music as she pranced about,
admiring herself.

Mr Wolf bowed his best royal bow and said,
"Your Royal Highness, a witch cast a spell on this prince.
Please will you kiss him better?"

"Get lost!" said the princess.
"I'm not kissing a slimy frog!"

"Perhaps I can tempt you with some turnip stew,"
said Mr Wolf, his tummy rumbling at the very thought of it . . .

"I don't want stew from the likes of you," scoffed the princess.

"Never mind her," said the cat with the fiddle.
"She's awfully vain. But what about me?
I'm a *royal* cat. You can trace
my ancestry right back
to the Egyptians. For a
bowl of turnip stew,
I'll kiss him better."

Everyone agreed it was worth a try.
So, the cat kissed the frog.

NOTHING HAPPENED.

"Oh no!" cried the frog. "I am doomed to be froggy for ever."

"Don't give up," said the cat.
"She's not our only princess. Follow me."

The second princess was relaxing in
the palace gardens.
Mr Wolf bowed his best royal bow.
"Your Royal Highness," he said.
"A cruel witch cast a spell
on this handsome prince.
Please, *please* will you kiss
him better?"

"He'll give you some of his
turnip stew," added the frog.

"Can't you see I'm busy?" shouted the princess.
"Anyway, I *hate* turnip stew."

"Don't mind her," said the servant goose.
"She's very lazy. But how about me?
I'm a *royal* goose.
I can lay golden eggs.
For a bowl of turnip stew,
I'll kiss him."

So, the goose kissed the frog.

AND ABSOLUTELY NOTHING HAPPENED.

The frog was very upset.
"Cheer up," said the goose. "Follow me to the royal garage."

But the garage was cold and grimy, and
quite empty except for a girl in overalls
tinkering with a car.
"This is no place to find a princess!"
grumbled the frog. Mr Wolf's tummy
rumbled. He looked closely at the girl.

She wasn't very fancy, but she was a princess!

Mr Wolf bowed his best royal bow (he was getting rather good at it now) and said, "Your Royal Highness! A nasty, wicked witch cast a spell on this delightful, charming prince. Please, please, *please*, kiss him better."

The princess blew her nose on an oily rag.
"What's in it for me?" she said.
"A delicious bowl of turnip stew!" replied Mr Wolf.
"I love turnip stew!" said the princess.
"Yum, yum!"

"You don't look like
a princess to me," said the frog.

**"Hush up, frog,
and hold still!"**
commanded the princess.

. . . SHAZAM!

There stood a handsome prince.
He was absolutely splendid.

Mr Wolf was very impressed.

"Your Royal Highness,
Mr Prince, Sir,"
he said politely,
"now it's your turn
to help me."

"Oh, no," said the prince.
"It's simply not done for a noble prince to be seen
consorting with common wolves
and grubby old turnips.
Out of my way,
before I throw you
in my dungeons!"

"What a waste of a kiss," said the princess, in disgust.
"And still no turnip stew," said Mr Wolf.

It was time for drastic action.
Mr Wolf telephoned the witch
who had made the spell.

"We're having problems with our prince," he said. "He's *mean* and *nasty* and he doesn't keep his promises."

"I know," replied the witch. "That's why I magicked him in the first place."

"Can't you change him back?" asked Mr Wolf.

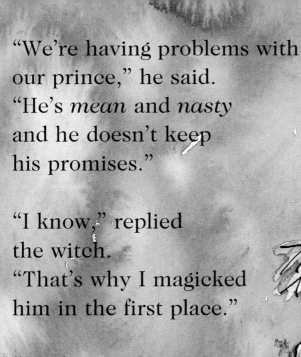

"Sorry," said the witch. "I'm afraid you are stuck with him."

FREE TROLL
WITH EVERY
BROOM SOLD!

NO REFUNDS
NO RETURNS
~~~~~~~~~~
ALL SPELLS
SOLD AS SEEN
~~~~~~~~~~
So be careful
what you
wish for!

BOGEYMAN
SALE!
(slightly soiled)

HUBBLE
BUBBLE
COUGH
DROPS

HOCUS
POCUS
Computers

"Oh, no," sighed Mr Wolf.
"Oh, no!" shrieked the princess.
"Those rascals are stealing my car!"

Mr Wolf thought very hard for a moment.
There was only one decent thing to do.

HE GOBBLED THE ROTTEN PRINCE UP!
And the horrid princesses, too!

SNAPPETY!

SNAP!

SNAP!

"Good riddance to the lot of them," said the nice princess,
and she gave Mr Wolf a big hug and a . . .

"Now let's go and pick that turnip!" said Mr Wolf.

Together, Mr Wolf and his new friends *pulled* and *tugged*, *heaved* and *huffed*. And finally . . .

POP!

. . . out came the turnip!

There was plenty of spicy stew for everyone.
And even though he'd already had a right royal feast,
Mr Wolf had an extra big helping.

Yum, yum!